Dedicated to Our Mams & Dads

Published by Dbee Press
8 New Row, Belvedere, Mullingar, Co. Westmeath, Ireland
Text copyright © Dolores Keaveney 2017
Illustration copyright © Keaveny & Lennon Children 2017
Design & Layout by Gary Kelly

www.doloreskeaveney.com

ISBN: 978-0-9571917-9-2

DILLY

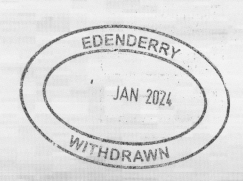

THE CAMPER

& The Magic Fairy Garden

Dilly The Camper
Finds A New Home

Once upon a time there was a very lonely camper. Because it had been lying in a small garden it was very neglected and run down. It was covered with leaves and mud and it had lots of green sticky moss growing on it. The rain was pouring in and it was a very sad sight indeed.

It had been a very nice camper once and had brought the family on wonderful trips to magic places. The family had all grown up and forgotten about it. Nobody wanted it and it was left to rot.

One day a Grandad named John called to see his old friend Digger who was the owner of the camper. They had been friends for a long time. After tea they went for a walk and as they passed the camper John looked at it and said to Digger, 'That is a very sad looking sight, isn't it'. 'Yes it is', replied Digger, 'would you like to take it, because I am finished with it? If you don't want it I will have to take it to the dump'. John looked at the camper and thought 'well maybe'. Suddenly he had dreams of fixing it. He could see himself at the seaside with his grandchildren, or taking it fishing, or even to a rock concert. He turned to Digger and said, 'I would love to be the owner of a camper.'

'I will try to start it', said Digger to John. 'You will have no luck there', John replied. Digger got the keys and put them in the ignition. He turned the key and to his amazement it started with one turn. The camper was delighted because it knew it was going to a new home and that maybe the new owner would clean it up and fix it.

John drove it to his home. When they arrived the camper saw a beautiful house and it knew that it would have a lovely life here.

Grandchildren Name The Camper

Just then some of John's grandchildren called unexpectedly. There was Lizzy, Gregory, Billy, Malaki, Alice, Marita, Huwie and A.J. When the children saw the camper they all thought that it looked very bad. John told them about his plans and how he was going to clean and renovate it. They jumped inside and had a look around. 'Maybe it is not so bad after all', they thought.

The children decided that it needed a name. So they called it DILLY and they all agreed that this name was a great one and the camper also agreed that it was the loveliest name it had ever heard.

John soon got working on it. With the help of all his grandchildren he spent many long days cleaning and repairing all the broken parts. He fixed the floor, painted and decorated it, painted lovely flowers on the walls and made it very comfortable.

Blossom The Magic Fairy Appears

One day the children were inside colouring at a small table. Alice dropped her crayon on the floor underneath the table. She bent down to pick it up when suddenly a very small person with wings appeared from a hole in the floor. It looked like a fairy. In fact it was a fairy. The children were startled for a moment but the little fairy spoke to them and said, 'Hello, my name is BLOSSOM, and I live in a magic fairy garden just a step away from here. I have come for your help, because our magic fairy garden will no longer be here if we do not find our beautiful magic crystal called the ETERNAL EYE which has been stolen from us.

Can you please come with me now to my home and help all of us find it'? she asked. 'We have until 12 o'clock tonight to find the quartz crystal and replace it or this garden will no longer exist'. The children did not know what to do because they could not disappear from home for hours, but in this magic garden time did not matter, and an hour could be just one minute in human time, so they decided to help the fairies.

The children were very excited and said they would come right away. They had never seen a fairy home before. They really believed in fairies but had never ever seen one, and there, right in front of them, was one standing and they were not going to miss the opportunity to see a fairy home, so they decided to go. BLOSSOM waved her little magic wand and shrunk all the children so that they could fit through the little hole in the floor.

One by one down they went through the hole and they were amazed to find themselves inside a world which they did not know existed. The place was beautiful. There were flowers, trees, rivers and streams everywhere. The whole place glittered and twinkled and there were fairies of all shapes and sizes to be seen. BLOSSOM introduced them to her best friends, Daisy, Foxglove, Lily and Poppy and lots more, and all of the fairies were named after flowers.

'Come', they said, and the children followed their new young friends down through the magical home. They walked on and on until they were in a beautiful fairy garden, full to the brim with flowers of every shape and size. They could see lots and lots of fairy houses dotted around the garden. The houses were all shaped like flowers. They could see a cherry blossom house, and this was where Blossom the fairy lived. They saw a daisy house, a poppy house and lots and lots more.

The fairies flew through the garden, gliding and twirling through the flowers and trees. They sat on the daisies, hid in the foxgloves and under the toadstools. There seemed to be magic everywhere and soon the children found that they too could fly around as if they were fairies. They also could talk to the fairies in a fairy language. They could speak to the animals and birds and could understand everything that was said.

Meeting The Magical Birds, Bee And Animals

They met BEELICIOUS BEE. She was a very magical bee who had a very strong sting. She had golden stripes along her body and she buzzed here and there around the magic garden. They also met RUTHIE ROBIN who was also a magic little robin bird. She could turn herself into a giant robin when she wanted to and she had four magical wings.

They met DIANA DUCK, a duck with magical powers. She wore a crown on her head and she also had special fairy wings. She wore a beautiful cerise pink dress and a pair of yellow boots.

She told the children that all they had to do was to whistle a magic tune which she whispered to Gregory and she would come immediately to help out. These little magic creatures would help the children later in their adventures. This garden was so special that they wished they could stay forever. The children did not realise that there was something very wrong in the beautiful garden.

The fairies told them the whole story. The garden had been there for thousands of years and all the fairies lived very happily there. They told the children that at the very end of the magic garden lay a very big and beautiful crystal stone. This stone was very big and was put there thousands of years ago when the garden was created.

In the centre of this large crystal stone lay a smaller blue and black crystal in the shape of a very large beautiful eye. This was called the ETERNAL EYE and it could see everything that was happening in the universe and as long as it was placed in the centre of the large crystal this magic little fairy garden would exist for eternity. The fairies knew that if this stone were ever taken out then the magical fairy garden and everyone in it would disappear forever.

They told the children that on this very day someone had stolen the crystal eye from the stone. So the children set off to find the magic crystal.

Before they went the fairies told them a secret song. If this song was heard across the garden then all the little fairies knew that someone was in danger and they could trace the music to where it was coming from. They told the children that if they found the crystal they were all to sing the secret song loudly.

Dilly Dilly da
Dilly Dilly dee

SEARCHING FOR
THE ETERNAL EYE

They all split up into groups, and went to different locations. They searched and searched. They looked everywhere. Lizzy, Alice, Marita and A.J. searched among the woods. These were such magical woods. All of the trees had faces and could speak. They flew up through the trees and down to the streams. They lifted up stones and searched there. While they were in the wood they came to a clearing where there were no trees. Lots of little animals ran around and out of nowhere appeared a little deer. This little deer had huge antlers that reached up into the air. It ran and jumped with delight. The children joined in and had great fun playing

with it. 'My name is ORCHID', it said, 'and I have magic powers. Would you like to see'? 'Yes', they replied. Suddenly there in front of their eyes it became a beautiful pink unicorn. They gazed in amazement as the beautiful unicorn danced all around the woods.

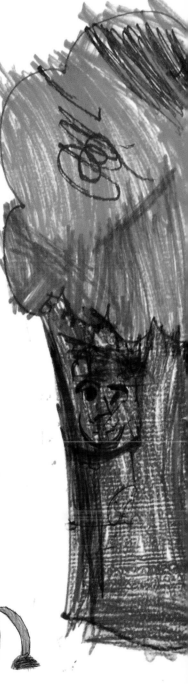

Just then a very wise old fairy appeared. Her name was NOLI. She had been living in this magic fairy garden for a very long time. She looked after all the baby fairies and played with them every day. The children told ORCHID and NOLI all about the stolen crystal. NOLI told them not to worry and to make sure to look everywhere. After playing with her and the unicorn for some time they continued their search through the woods. But to their dismay they could not find the crystal.

MEETING BOBBY THE HARE

The other four children, Gregory, Billy, Malaki and Huwie went further and further out into the magic garden. They ran and ran until they came to a crossroads. They did not know what way to turn. They started to argue among themselves. 'We will take this road', said Gregory. 'No we won't', said Billy. 'Why not take this road'? said Malaki and Huwie as they pointed at the road to the right. They were shouting at one another when suddenly out of nowhere a very large life-sized hare appeared.

27

The children were startled and they could not believe what they were seeing before their eyes. It was the biggest hare they had ever seen and it was dressed in the most colourful outfit. It wore purple pants, a bright red waistcoat, a yellow shirt, a green dickey-bow and it had an enormous red hat on its head. It was carrying a rainbow-coloured walking stick. 'My name is BOBBY THE HARE' it said. 'What is going on here? Why are you all shouting and arguing'? The children told the hare about the beautiful magic fairy garden, about the fairies and about the missing crystal ETERNAL EYE. 'Oh no, this is dreadful. I know about a creature that has been searching for this crystal all over the universe. I hope that the crystal has not been taken by that creature. This is a very bad thing to have happened', he said.

BOBBY THE HARE told the children to be nice and kind to one another and to stop arguing. 'I will come and help you find the crystal', he said. The children were delighted because they were getting unsure as to what to do next and time was running out.

MORE MAGICAL CREATURES

On their journey they met many different animals.   They met BROADFEET THE GREYHOUND and SAM THE TERRIER, two lovely dogs that were playing games with one another.   They said that they had not seen anything suspicious, so the children and BOBBY THE HARE continued on searching.

They came to a small cottage with lots of birds singing and nesting in the small trees that grew around it. Here lived a woman called CHRISA. She noticed that the children were very tired looking so she asked them to come in for a rest. She was a very funny woman and she dressed funny also. She wore a long polka-dot dress and had flowers in her hair. She entertained them with lots of stories and jokes. They laughed and laughed until their sides ached.

She made them some lovely lemonade from the lemons that grew on the trees outside her house. She told them about her pet dinosaur. 'It will take you to the big cave where you can search for the crystal', she said.

The dinosaur took them to a very large cave at the side of a stream. The children noticed a very strange roadway which was coloured red and black and right at the end of this roadway was a large cave with a gigantic red alien-type giant sitting at the entrance. The children knew that this was not the cave they were trying to find and they ran past it at great speed. They did not want to have anything to do with the red alien-type giant. So they went on just a little bit further down the red road.

MAGIC FAIRY MOLLY

Soon they came upon a very large cave with a huge boulder blocking the entrance. 'Oh dear', said Gregory. 'That is a huge boulder'. It was blocking the entrance to the cave. 'It will take a lot of magic to shift that', said BOBBY THE HARE. The children sat down on the ground and felt very tired. They knew that it would be almost impossible for them to move that boulder

Suddenly a beautiful fairy called MOLLY stood right in front of the very large boulder. 'Hello everybody', said FAIRY MOLLY. 'Are you all in a spot of bother'? 'Yes we are', said the children. 'We need to get into the cave to search for the ETERNAL EYE rose quartz crystal which has been

stolen from the fairy garden.　There is no way that we could ever get into this cave without moving the large stone'.

FAIRY MOLLY said she was the wishing fairy and could grant them a wish. So they all wished that the big stone would move and that they would be able to get inside. FAIRY MOLLY said some magic words and suddenly the large stone moved away and left enough room for everyone to go inside. The children and BOBBY THE HARE were very grateful and thanked FAIRY MOLLY from the bottom of their hearts and told her they would love to meet her again. She told them that they had two more wishes and that they were to call on her if they ever needed her help. They were so delighted to hear this and told FAIRY MOLLY that they would surely need her again. So they said goodbye and in they went and continued down a very narrow dark passage.

Suddenly they couldn't see a thing and could not find their way back. 'FAIRY MOLLY, FAIRY MOLLY', they called. We are here inside the cave but we cannot see a thing and we cannot even see our way back out'. FAIRY MOLLY appeared with a gigantic sparkling light which was a great help to the children and BOBBY THE HARE.

They continued further and further into the cave. From deep in the cave they could hear something making a very strange sound. They crept very slowly and silently on until they came to a very large opening inside the heart of the cave. Gregory, Malaki, Huwie and Billy were very surprised to see a very large crystal eye staring straight at them. It was lying in the centre of the cave right on top of a very large rock. They were very excited to see it and know that if they could only get to it they would be able to save the magic garden and the entire little fairy family.

CRANKY THE CROCK AND DIANA DUCK

The crystal eye was surrounded by a river of water and inside in this river lived a very large crocodile called CRANKY who stuck up his head and snapped his very large sharp teeth SNAP SNAP at them, and the children knew that if they were to bring the crystal back then they would have to cross the river to get to it.

They knew that this was a very dangerous thing to do and remembered their parents' advice never to get into a river on their own without an adult present.

Snap

Gregory said "Why don't we call on DIANA DUCK for help? After all she told us to call on her any time we needed her help". So Gregory whistled the magic tune and DIANA DUCK appeared on the river and used her magic. She quacked a secret quack that changed the water into rock, leaving a very small little pond for CRANKY THE CROCK to stay safe and sound. BOBBY THE HARE and the children walked straight across without delay. They made it. They climbed up on top of the very large rock and they all bent down to lift the crystal.

NOGARD APPEARS

Suddenly they heard a terrorising scream and right there underneath their feet in front of their very eyes was the ugliest creature they had ever seen. The creature had disguised himself as a very large rock just like the rocks all around and the children had mistaken it for a real rock and climbed on top of it. Gregory, Malaki, Huwie and Billy were terrified and let out a scream 'HELP, HELP, Fairy Molly'. FAIRY MOLLY appeared once again as promised with their final wish. She lifted all the children down from the back of the creature just in the nick of time. They were very thankful.

BOBBY THE HARE had already jumped down himself with no trouble. He told the children that this was indeed the creature and it was called a NOGARD. It had one enormous eye in the centre of its forehead. It had roamed the universe for thousands and thousands of years looking for the ETERNAL EYE.

They were frozen to the ground and tried to turn around and run but could not. The creature howled and screeched and told the children that he would devour them in one gulp. He said that the crystal eye was now his and he needed it to give him the greatest power in the world and he would live forever once he had the crystal in place.

The children knew that they had to get the crystal eye no matter what happened and they knew that if they did not do it soon that they would never see their sisters and brothers and cousins or their parents ever again.

FAIRIES TO THE RESCUE

The children remembered when they were in the fairy garden and had met the fairies who gave them the magic secret song. They had told them to sing it loudly if they were in trouble and they would all come to help. So the children started to sing the secret song which everyone in the fairy flower garden knew.

Dilly Dilly da Dilly Dilly **Dee,**

I'm **in trouble,** please help me.

I need help **from someone strong,**

All you **fairies** hear my song.

They sang loud and clear, their voices travelled through the air and they could be heard for miles and miles. The fairies knew they were needed. Suddenly hundreds and hundreds of fairies and little people of all shapes and sizes and the rest of the children, Lizzy, Alice, Marita and A.J., came soaring through the big cave with lighted candles.

They zoomed down on top of the ugly creature. They prodded and poked it with their lighted candles. The ugly creature roared with anger but the little people just kept prodding and poking it. Suddenly BEELICIOUS BEE arrived and swooped down on top of the NOGARD and knocked it out with its magic sting.

BOBBY THE HARE poked the creature in the eye socket with his rainbow walking stick and dislodged the crystal eye. It popped out and rolled along the ground. All of the children helped each other to grab the crystal eye. They carefully lifted it out of the cave.

RUTHIE ROBIN TO THE RESCUE

RUTHIE ROBIN arrived and with her magic powers turned herself into the biggest robin the children ever saw. She flapped her extra set of fairy wings and the children were able to jump up on her back with the crystal ETERNAL EYE and RUTHIE ROBIN flew all of them back to the large crystal stone with BOBBY THE HARE holding on to her tail.

They looked at the magic clock and realised that they had just one minute to get the eye into the crystal.   They pushed and pushed and in it went. All of the fairies and fairy folk let out a huge cheer of delight. They ran up and hugged the children.   They were so happy and grateful.

GRANDAD CALLING

Suddenly the children heard their Grandad calling and the spell was broken and they found themselves back in the camper with just BLOSSOM the fairy. They all said a quick farewell to her. Blossom told the children that she would introduce them to lots of magical creatures when they came back on their next visit to their Grandad.

The children were delighted to know that they would meet again with all the new friends that they had met on their adventure. 'What are you all doing in there'? called Grandad John. 'Just playing and colouring', they all replied. The children looked at each other and traced their fingers across their lips, which meant 'shush, don't tell'.

They all came outside and continued to help their Grandad John clean and polish DILLY but they knew that this was no ordinary camper and that it was just the beginning of their adventures. It was truly magical and they knew that there would be many more amazing and exciting visits to the magic fairy garden ahead with BLOSSOM and her fairy family.

Grandad John was very happy with the work and he had lots of trips planned for the future. He would take all the children to the seaside. They could go swimming and make sandcastles. He would take them fishing. He would go to a rock concert. He dreamt of all the places he would go.

GRANDAD JOHN MEETS HIS OLD FRIEND DIGGER AGAIN

One day John brought DILLY THE CAMPER back to visit his old friend Digger. Digger could hardly believe his eyes when he saw her. He looked at John and said, 'What a brilliant job you have done'.

Digger said to John, 'I am now a very happy man, because I know that the camper I loved has been restored, and I know it will bring magical journeys and great surprises to you and to your grandchildren and to whoever travels in it'.

DILLY, the children and the fairies knew it would.

THE END

THE STORY OF THE BOOK

This book is a joint project between me and my grandchildren.

While I wrote the outline of the book, all of the children put the magic into the story by creating the monster, fairies, animals and the crystal eye. They called to visit on a regular basis over the past two years and on every occasion took out the paper and crayons and drew and coloured a character for the book. By the end of this two year period 'HEY PRESTO' they had all of the illustrations completed, and with a bit of tweaking of the story, Dilly the Camper and the Magic Fairy Garden came to life.

The Illustrators are:

Ellie Keaveney

Greg Keaveney

Mal Keaveney

Will Lennon

Ali Lennon

Marta Lennon

Hue Keaveney

Austin Keaveney

I hope you enjoy the story and illustrations and just remember that in fairyland everything is possible.

Bobby the Hare

If you like this book, you'll love..